# The Little Red Hen

Penny Dolan and Beccy Blake

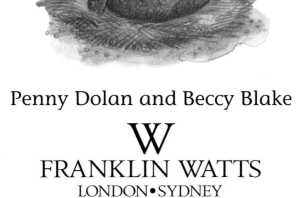

W
FRANKLIN WATTS
LONDON•SYDNEY

Little Red Hen found some grains of wheat but she did not gobble them up. "If these seeds were planted," she thought, "they'd grow into lots more wheat."

So Little Red Hen told Cat, Dog
and Rat. The friends agreed it
was a good plan.
"Will you help me plant
the wheat?" she asked.

"Not I," said Cat. "I'm scratching my fur."

"Not I," said Dog. "I'm finding a bone."

"Not I," said Rat. "I'm busy."

Little Red Hen would not give up.
"I will just have to do it myself,"
she decided.

Wheat

She found a
patch of ground
and planted
those grains.

The Ratty
Times

7

The rain fell, the sun shone and the seeds grew. So did the weeds.

"Who will help me clear away the weeds?" asked Little Red Hen.

"Not I!" Cat just smiled.

"Not I!" Dog just grinned.

"Not I!" said Rat, laughing.

Little Red Hen would not give up.

"I will do it myself!" she said.

She pulled and tugged until all

the weeds had gone.

Summer came. The green wheat became golden and ripe.

11

It was time to harvest the wheat.
Little Red Hen found her friends
under a shady tree.
"Who will help me to cut the wheat?"
she enquired.

"Not I!" yawned Cat. "I'm too hot."

"Not I!" yawned Dog. "I'm too tired."

"Not I!" yawned Rat.

"Too much work."

However, the Little Red Hen
was determined.

"I will do it myself," she said.

Swish, swish! She cut the wheat and tied it into sheaves.

Then it was time for the wheat to go
to the windmill.

"Who will help me carry the wheat?"
Little Red Hen asked.

"Not I!" grumbled Cat, crossly.

"Not I!" grumbled Dog, angrily.

"Not I!" grumbled Rat. "Stop
bothering us!"

Little Red Hen sighed.
"Then I'll take the
wheat up to the
windmill myself,"
she said.

18

The wind turned round the sails of the mill, and they turned round the machine inside the mill, and the heavy grindstones ground the grains into fine flour.

Little Red Hen got everything ready.
"Who will help me make the bread?"
asked Little Red Hen.

Nobody answered. Cat, Dog
and Rat were asleep.
"Then I'll make and bake the loaf
myself!" she said with a sigh.

Cat's ears twitched. Dog's ears sniffed.

Rat suddenly felt very hungry.

What was that delicious smell?

22

Little Red Hen was holding a crusty
golden loaf.

"Who will help me eat my
bread?" she called.

Cat, Dog and Rat ran to her side.

"Me!" said Cat.

"Me!" said Dog,

"Me, me, me!" said Rat.

Little Red Hen looked surprised.
"What do you three want? I grew the
wheat myself. I made the bread myself.
None of you helped."

"But you have far too much
bread to eat yourself!"
they told her.

Little Red Hen laughed.

"Oh, I'm not eating it by myself," she told them. "Look! Here come my happy little chicks. They will help me eat up all my bread."

And that is exactly what happened.

# About the story

*The Little Red Hen* is an old folk tale that is believed to have come from Russia. It became very popular, especially in America. The story is still used for its moral of working hard if you want something in return. It is often compared to Aesop's fable *The Ant and the Grasshopper,* which also features hardworking and lazy animals. Often, the other animals featured include a pig and a duck.

# Be in the story!

Imagine you are
the Little Red Hen.
How do you feel when
the other animals don't
want to help you?

Now imagine you
are Dog, Cat or Rat.
How do you feel
when Little Red Hen
won't share her bread?
Do you think you deserve any?

First published in 2014 by
Franklin Watts
338 Euston Road
London
NW1 3BH

Franklin Watts Australia
Level 17/207 Kent Street
Sydney
NSW 2000

A CIP catalogue record for this book is available
from the British Library.

The artwork for this story first appeared in
Leapfrog: The Little Red Hen

ISBN 978 1 4451 2851 1 (hbk)
ISBN 978 1 4451 2852 8 (pbk)
ISBN 978 1 4451 2854 2 (library ebook)
ISBN 978 1 4451 2853 5 (ebook)

Series Editor: Jackie Hamley
Series Advisor: Catherine Glavina
Series Designer: Cathryn Gilbert

Printed in China

Franklin Watts is a divison of
Hachette Children's Books,
an Hachette UK company.
www.hachette.co.uk